Voices
of the
Wild

Voices of the Wild

by Jonathan London
illustrated by Wayne McLoughlin

CROWN PUBLISHERS, INC.
New York

I am Beaver gliding,
diving
        rising with the bubbles
to a long, slender shadow-shape
passing overhead. A man
in a kayak paddles, pauses . . .
I slap tail and dive again,
but the man glides
one with the river.
        I surface
and we glide together
in the long silence
of the northern summer sunrise.

I am Bear scavenging
among the man's things.
There is food here in the ashes
of his campfire, and more —
I sniff it on the air
                    nearby.
But he comes, his kayak
sliding in, his paddle raised,
his voice, in a shout:
GET OUT! GET OUT!
I rear up, stand tall,
all claws and teeth
                    ROARRR!
He slaps water and yells and I —
I scratch the white moon
on my belly, yawn
                    and amble off
to look for berries.

I am Deer stepping
through the crisp shadows,
twitching ears against deerflies,
stretching my neck
to whatever tastes good.

I hear steps
downwind.
Nothing to smell.
Nothing moves.

Then I see the man, part of the trees.
We are two pairs of eyes
meeting in the stillness.
Two hearts
           beating
in the silence.

I am Turtle
down under . . .
water is my world
and sun. How I love to sun
on a log and snooze
the long afternoon
                    away.
But I hear a ripple,
a paddle touch my world,
and I flop with a small plop
back in, swim among reeds
and watch the man searching for me,
wishing to see
a turtle on a log
                    in the sun.

I am Moose nuzzling
in the ooze
of the shallows, snorting,
and I am HUNGRY
for juicy roots and tender tendrils.

Around the bend
comes the man in a kayak.
Too close, too close.
I raise my huge snout, dripping,
my great flat antlers
hanging torn green stems
                and stomp water.
He back-paddles
to a safe distance. He knows
Moose likes space.
I eat.

I am Eagle soaring,
                    circling.
From here the man is tiny.
My eye is sharp
and I see the fish he caught.
I pierce the air
with my scream.
                    My shadow
slides over him. Talons down,
I grip the air he breathes. His fish
escapes from him —
but not from me.
Where sky meets water
I am king.

I am Otter, utterly
in love with life.
I delight in tumbling water,
the spin and sheen of light
gleaming in my fur. The
                    whoosh
and slide of sound
in my under-water ears.

What's that? Something coming.
I love my life too much to lose it.
Something in my blood's memory
warns me to flee. The man will only see
a quick, sleek movement among stones —
and I am gone.

I am Dipper, or Water Ouzel.
My nest is a ball of moss on a rock wall.
But my home is the water.
Give me a rushing, mountain stream
and I am in it in a flash.
I dive. I swim under water.
I walk on the bottom.
Give me a mayfly larva or a tiny trout
and I will snatch it,
                    and eat.
When I come out to dry my feathers
the man is there, watching.
I bob up and down on a wet boulder,
dip, dip, dip.
I sing *zeet, zeet, zeet*.
Then I walk back in the water
                    and keep on walking.
From below, the man is a shadow flowing
and standing still at the same time.

I am Lynx.
I pad softly through deep grass,
crouch, with muscles bunched —
                    and *pounce*.
Paws shoot sharp claws, and mouse
cannot escape
                    this time.
But then I hear a branch snap. My ears
swivel. I crouch again. Through the blades,
the man stands. I gaze into the sun-glow,
low and blood-red behind him.
I am not afraid, just cautious.
I wait. The river mumbles
and mutters in the distance.
Then I ripple like wind through the grass —
half a mouse dangling — toward the dark woods.
I am quiet as the approaching night.

I am Loon floating
on a cool lake.
I dive down deep one more time
and come up with a flopping, flapping fish
in my daggerlike bill.
                    Swallow.
The full moon is rising,
spilling molten gold on dark water.
The dip and splash of a paddle,
and I know the man is near. He means
no harm. Not this one.
But I dive down, swim, and pop up silently
in another spot, just to keep him looking.
Then I cry my yodeling call —
my lonely wail
for a long-lost mate —
                    and take off
running on water, thrashing white
in the golden light.

I am Wolf. I am not alone.
I tumble in the twilight
with my little ones. They tug
my ears, my nose, my tail
                    and yelp
when I nip. They snarl and grunt
and crawl all over me.
                    Afterwards
we lick each other's fur. We are family.
But now it is time for the hunt.
We have smelled the man near here,
and seen him once, inspecting our tracks.
But he does not come close.
This is our place.
We announce our presence to other packs
and fill the night with our howls.
We are coming.

I am Owl gliding
through low branches.
I settle on a limb
and blink slow in the moonlight.
I do not need this light to see,
and I see all, hear all.
Tiny movements underground,
under mushrooms and moss.
                The man
snoring near the dying fire.
I hoot three times.
The man stirs.
I am a dream that takes flight,
silent as the moon.
I float low for the slightest sound.
There!

I am Beaver
      Bear
      Deer
      Turtle
      Moose
      Eagle
      Otter
      Dipper
      Lynx
      Loon
      Wolf
      Owl

I am all of these
      . . . and I am the man.

When I wake in the dark
easy on the earth
and see the shape of an owl
       among the stars
I lift my voice to the silence
and give thanks
to the wild night.

For the wordless of the wild

with thanks to fellow kayakers Roger Ledbetter and Lisa Thompson,

and Mary TallMountain, poet

—J. L.

For my daughter, Allison Laurel,

and Jackie, my wife and my best friend

— W. M.

Published by Crown Publishers, Inc., a Random House company, 201 East 50th Street,
New York, New York 10022

CROWN is a trademark of Crown Publishers, Inc.

Manufactured in the United States of America

Library of Congress Cataloging-in-Publication Data
London, Jonathan. 1947–
Voices of the wild / by Jonathan London ; illustrated by Wayne McLoughlin.
p. cm.
Summary: Beaver, Bear, Deer, and other animals speak about their lives in the wild and their
relationship with humans.
1. Animals—Juvenile fiction. [1. Animals—Fiction. 2. Man—Influence on nature—Fiction.] I.
McLoughlin, Wayne, ill. II. Title
PZ10.3.L8534Vo 1993
[Fic]—dc20   92-27651

ISBN 0-517-59217-7 (trade)
0-517-59218-5 (lib. bdg.)

10 9 8 7 6 5 4 3 2 1   FIRST EDITION